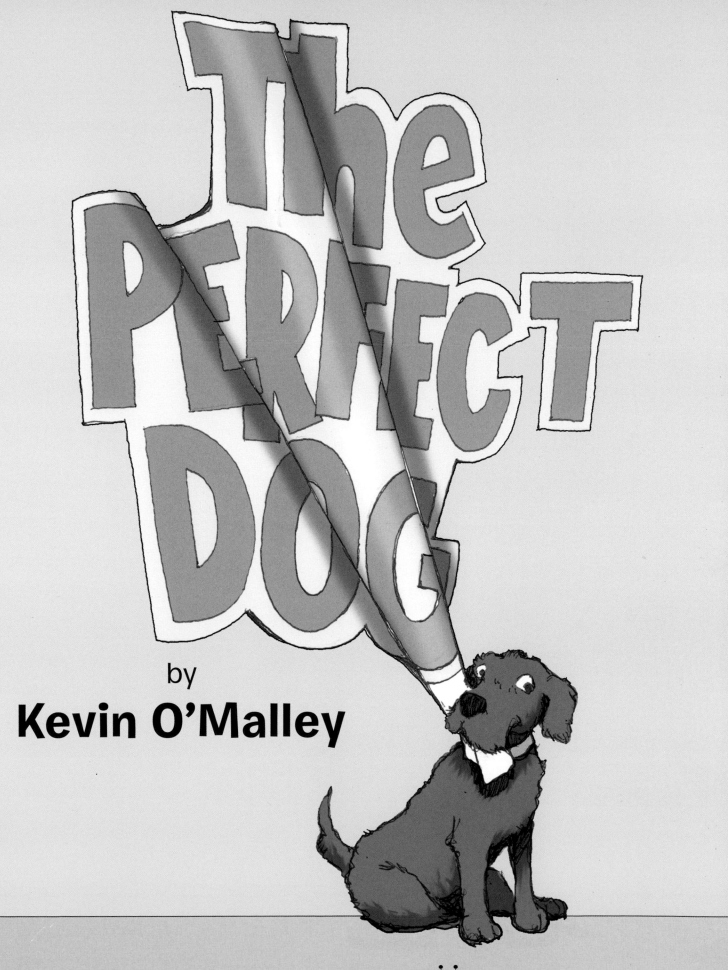

The PERFECT DOG

by

Kevin O'Malley

Crown Books for Young Readers ♛ New York

FOR DARA, WHO HAS THE PERFECT DOG

Visit us on the Web! randomhousekids.com
Educators and librarians, for a variety of teaching tools,
visit us at RHTeachersLibrarians.com

Library of Congress Cataloging-in-Publication Data
Names: O'Malley, Kevin, 1961– author, illustrator.
Title: The perfect dog / Kevin O'Malley.
Description: First edition. | New York : Crown Books for Young Readers, [2016] | Summary:
"A girl tries to pick the perfect dog for her, but in the end, the right dog picks her"– Provided by publisher.
Identifiers: LCCN 2015029102 | ISBN 978-1-101-93441-8 (hardback) | ISBN 978-1-101-93442-5 (glb) |
ISBN 978-1-101-93443-2 (epub)
Subjects: | CYAC: Dogs–Fiction. | BISAC: JUVENILE FICTION / Animals / Dogs. |
JUVENILE FICTION / Animals / Pets. | JUVENILE FICTION / Concepts / Words.
Classification: LCC PZ7.O526 Pe 2016 | DDC [E]–dc23

The illustrations in this book were created with ink on Graphics 360 paper
with a Hunt nib and colored in Photoshop.

MANUFACTURED IN CHINA   10 9 8 7 6 5 4 3 2 1   First Edition
Random House Children's Books supports the
First Amendment and celebrates the right to read.

My parents said
we could get a dog.

And I know
the perfect
dog. . . .

The perfect dog should be **big**...

The perfect dog
should be small . . .

smaller . . .

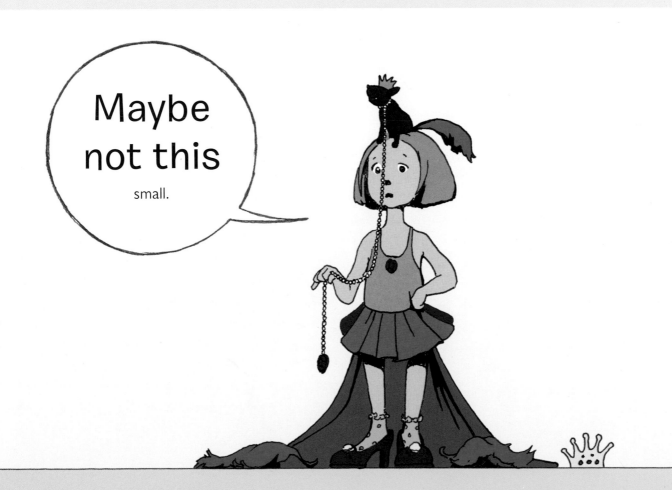

The perfect dog should have **LONG** hair...

LONGER...

The perfect dog should **NOT** be too...

Or too . . .

slobbery.

The perfect dog should be *fancy* . . .

fancier...

The perfect dog should be *fast*...

The perfect dog
should be

snuggly . . .

snugglier . . .

The perfect dog should **NOT** be too...

s l o-o-o w.

Or too . . .

So we went to get the perfect dog.

We finally decided the perfect dog should be . . .

But then . . .

The perfect dog found me!